Sometimes I Feel Like a Storm Cloud

The illustrations for this book were done in acrylics.
The text type for this book is Benguiat Frisky.

Text copyright © 1999 by Lezlie Evans
Illustrations copyright © 1999 by Marsha Gray Carrington

MONDO Publishing
One Plaza Road
Greenvale, New York 11548
MONDO is a registered trademark of Mondo Publishing
Visit our web site at http://www.mondopub.com

Printed in Hong Kong
99 00 01 02 03 04 05 06   HC   9 8 7 6 5 4 3 2 1
99 00 01 02 03 04 05 06   PB   9 8 7 6 5 4 3 2 1

Designed by David Neuhaus/NeuStudio
Production by The Kids at Our House

Library of Congress Cataloging-in-Publication Data
Evans, Lezlie.
Sometimes I feel like a storm cloud / by Lezlie Evans ; illustrated by Marsha Gray Carrington.
            p.   cm.
Summary: A child describes how it feels to experience a variety of emotions.
ISBN 1-57255-621-8 (hc : alk. paper).— ISBN 1-57255-622-6 (pbk. : alk. paper)
[1. Emotions—Fiction.]   I. Carrington, Marsha Gray, ill.   II. Title.
PZ7.E89115So   1999
[E]—dc21   98-3302
                                                                        CIP
                                                                        AC

To Nathan, my newest reason for feeling joy.—L.E.

For Robert, who always knew,
And Patti, who said just do it.—M.G.C.

Sometimes I Feel Like a Storm Cloud

by Lezlie Evans

illustrated by Marsha Gray Carrington

Sometimes I feel like a storm cloud—
a big, dark,
rumbling, grumbling
rain cloud,
ready to burst
into a shower of tears.

Sometimes I feel like a big balloon—
growing and growing,
so excited
that at any second

I might pop!

Sometimes I feel like a flattened balloon—
woooosh, smooosh,
with one big sigh
I've lost my air.

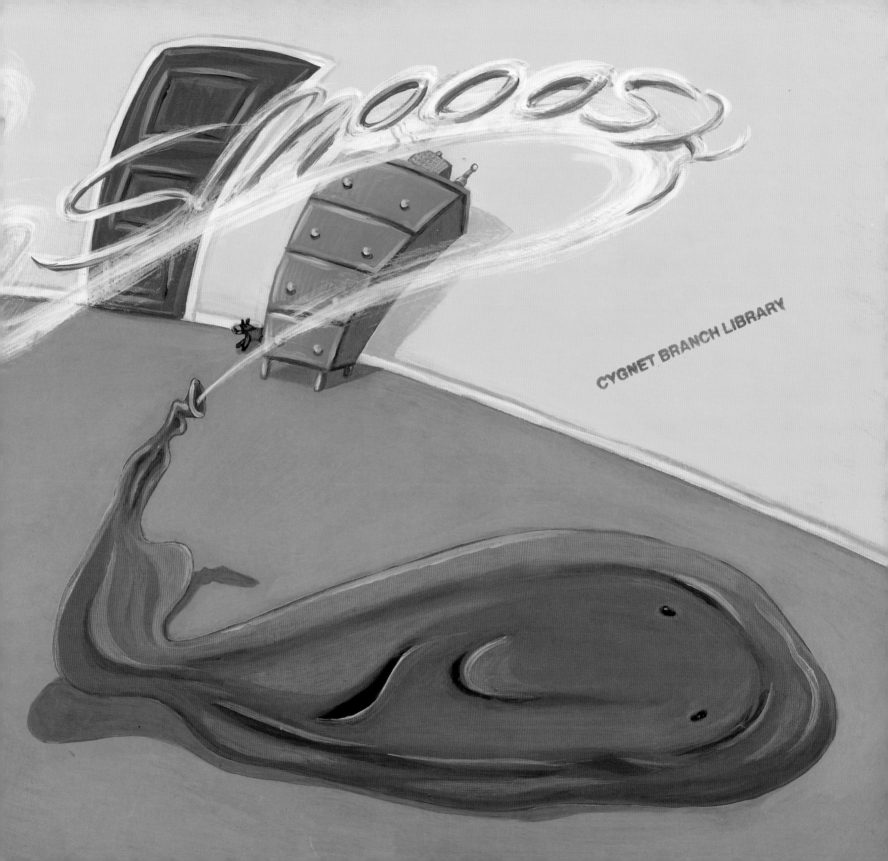

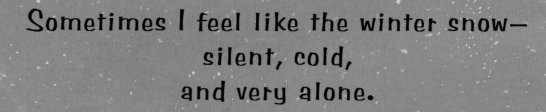

Sometimes I feel like the winter snow—
silent, cold,
and very alone.

Sometimes I feel like a newborn kitten—
tiny and timid,
wishing I was curled up
close to my mother.

Sometimes I feel like a race car—
revving my engine,
grrr-ripping, zzzip-zipping,
turning corners at high speeds.

Sometimes I feel like a peacock—
so big, so pleased
with what I can do.

Sometimes I feel like a tornado—
bashing, smashing
things to the ground;
blowing, throwing
things all around.

Sometimes I feel like a puppy dog—
delighted, excited,
circling around;
jumping, hugging,
eager to give kisses.

Sometimes I feel like a mighty bull—
huffing, puffing,
ready to charge.

Sometimes I feel like a fish—
splishing and splashing
while fanning my fins;
gliding and sliding
through the deepest oceans.

Sometimes I feel like a bear—
ready to take my winter nap.
Slow and sleepy,
I crawl toward my bed
and snuggle into
the cave of my covers.

Daddy gives me
a big bear hug
and turns out the light.
"Good night," he says,
and blows me a kiss.

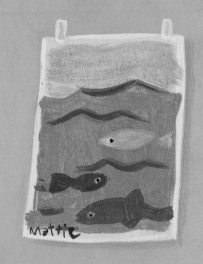

"Good night, Daddy," I whisper.